Divine Union; The Eternal Love Story of Shiva and Parvati

Mrigendra Bharti

Published by Sellbrochure Entertainment Vymish, 2024.

This is a work of fiction. Similarities to real people, places, or events are entirely coincidental.

DIVINE UNION; THE ETERNAL LOVE STORY OF SHIVA AND PARVATI

First edition. June 4, 2024.

Copyright © 2024 Mrigendra Bharti.

ISBN: 979-8227432223

Written by Mrigendra Bharti.

Table of Contents

Dedication

In the celestial realms where love reigns supreme, there exists a bond so pure and profound that it transcends the boundaries of time and space. It is the love story of Shiva and Parvati, a tale as old as creation itself, that has captivated the hearts of mortals and gods alike for eons.

To the Divine Couple, whose love knows no bounds and whose devotion knows no end,

In the cosmic dance of creation, you stand as eternal symbols of love's power to conquer all obstacles and unite souls in a bond that defies even the passage of time. From the sacred heights of Mount Kailash to the depths of the Cosmic Oceans, your love has illuminated the darkest corners of the universe and filled our hearts with awe and wonder.

With every glance exchanged and every touch shared, you have shown us the true meaning of devotion and selflessness. In your divine embrace, we find solace and inspiration, and in your unwavering commitment to each other, we see the eternal flame of love burning bright.

To Shiva, the lord of timeless grace, whose presence fills the heavens with divine light,

Your strength and wisdom guide us through the trials of life, and your compassion knows no bounds. In your eyes, we see the infinite depths of the cosmos, and in your heart, we find the courage to face our fears and overcome our doubts.

To Parvati, the goddess of beauty and grace, whose love illuminates the darkest night,

Your kindness and generosity nourish our souls, and your beauty radiates like the stars in the night sky. In your smile, we find hope and joy, and in your embrace, we find peace and serenity.

Together, you are the embodiment of divine love, the eternal union that binds us all in a tapestry of light and shadow. Your love story is a testament to the power of love to transform lives and transcend even the greatest of obstacles.

With deepest reverence and boundless gratitude,
Mrigendra Bharti

Preface

In the realm of Hindu mythology, few tales are as revered and cherished as the eternal love story of Lord Shiva and Goddess Parvati. It is a saga that transcends time and space, weaving together divine encounters, mortal trials, and profound teachings. Through their union, they embody the quintessence of love, devotion, and cosmic balance.

This book seeks to delve deep into the sacred bond between Shiva and Parvati, exploring its multifaceted dimensions and timeless relevance. Each chapter unfolds a chapter of their divine romance, revealing the intricacies of their relationship and the profound impact it has had on the universe.

As we embark on this journey through the annals of Hindu mythology, may we be inspired by the unwavering love and devotion of Shiva and Parvati, and may their timeless tale resonate in the depths of our souls.

Foreword

In the tapestry of Hindu mythology, the love story of Shiva and Parvati stands as a radiant thread, weaving together the celestial and the terrestrial, the divine and the mortal. It is a saga that captivates the hearts and minds of millions, transcending the boundaries of time and space.

As we delve into the pages of this book, we embark on a journey into the heart of this divine love epic. Through the sacred verses and timeless narratives, we are transported to the mystical realm of Mount Kailash, where the cosmic dance of Shiva and the gentle grace of Parvati intertwine in an eternal embrace.

Within these pages, we encounter not only the celestial romance of the divine couple but also the profound teachings and spiritual wisdom embedded within their love story. It is a tale of devotion, sacrifice, and transcendence, offering us invaluable insights into the nature of love and the essence of existence.

As we immerse ourselves in the pages that follow, may we be enriched by the wisdom of the ages and inspired by the timeless love of Shiva and Parvati, guiding us on a journey of self-discovery and spiritual awakening.

Prologue

In the sacred annals of Hindu mythology, amidst the celestial abodes of gods and goddesses, there exists a tale of love that transcends the boundaries of time and space. It is the story of Shiva, the eternal ascetic, and Parvati, the gentle goddess of beauty and devotion.

Long before the dawn of creation, when the cosmos lay shrouded in primordial darkness, Shiva, the Supreme Being, existed in profound meditation upon Mount Kailash. His solitary contemplation was disturbed only by the celestial strains of his divine consort, Parvati, who, unbeknownst to him, yearned for his companionship.

As the eons passed, Parvati's fervent devotion stirred the depths of Shiva's heart, drawing him irresistibly towards her. Thus began a timeless saga of love and longing, trials and triumphs, which continues to captivate the hearts of devotees and seekers alike.

In the pages that follow, we delve into the depths of this divine romance, unraveling the mysteries of Shiva and Parvati's sacred union and the profound significance it holds for humanity. Through their journey, we discover the essence of true love, the power of devotion, and the eternal dance of creation and destruction that sustains the universe.

Join us now, as we embark on a journey into the heart of Hindu mythology, where the love of Shiva and Parvati shines like a beacon of hope in the darkness, illuminating the path to spiritual awakening and eternal bliss.

Acknowledgment

In the endeavor to bring this book to fruition, I am grateful for the support and guidance of many individuals who have contributed their wisdom, encouragement, and expertise.

I extend my heartfelt gratitude to my readers, whose unwavering support and encouragement have been invaluable throughout this journey. Your feedback and enthusiasm have inspired me to delve deeper into the sacred tale of Shiva and Parvati, shaping this work into its present form.

I also express my appreciation to [List of people or entities], whose contributions in various capacities have helped shape this work into its present form. Their dedication and commitment to excellence have been instrumental in bringing this project to fruition.

Furthermore, I extend my gratitude to the countless devotees, scholars, and seekers of truth who have preserved and shared the timeless wisdom of Hindu mythology. It is through their devotion and reverence that the divine love story of Shiva and Parvati continues to resonate across the ages, inspiring countless souls on the path of spirituality and self-discovery.

Finally, I dedicate this book to the divine couple, Shiva and Parvati, whose eternal love and wisdom illuminate the path of righteousness and bliss for all beings.

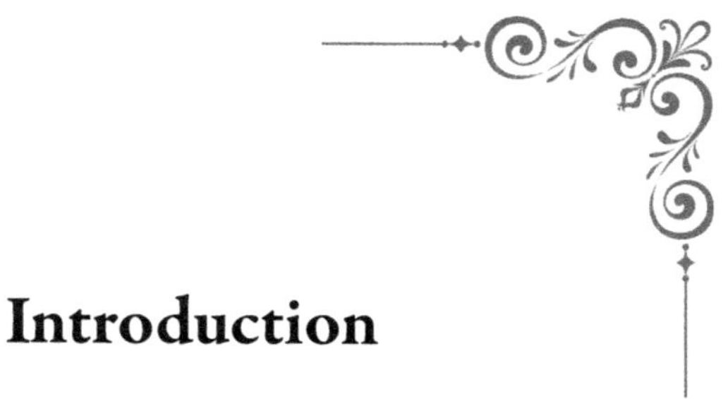

Introduction

In the heart of Hindu mythology lies a tale of love so profound, it transcends the boundaries of mortal existence and reaches into the very fabric of the universe. It is the timeless love story of Lord Shiva and Goddess Parvati, a divine saga that has captivated the hearts and minds of devotees for millennia.

In this book, we embark on a journey into the mystical realm of Mount Kailash, where the celestial dance of Shiva and the gentle grace of Parvati intertwine in an eternal embrace. Their love story, steeped in myth and legend, embodies the essence of devotion, sacrifice, and spiritual awakening.

Through the pages that follow, we delve into the depths of this divine romance, exploring the sacred encounters, trials, and triumphs that define the union of Shiva and Parvati. We unravel the mysteries of their celestial bond and uncover the profound teachings hidden within their love story.

But this book is not merely a retelling of ancient myths; it is a timeless journey of self-discovery and spiritual awakening. As we immerse ourselves in the divine love of Shiva and Parvati, we are reminded of the eternal truths that lie at the core of existence – the interconnectedness of all beings, the power of devotion, and the boundless nature of love.

Join us now, as we embark on a journey into the heart of
Hindu mythology, where the love of Shiva and Parvati shines
like a beacon of hope in the darkness, guiding us towards the
path of enlightenment and eternal bliss.

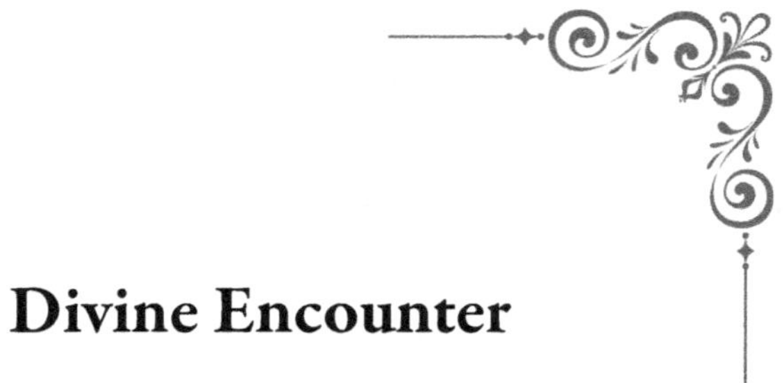

Divine Encounter

Meeting on Mount Kailash

In the timeless realm of Hindu mythology, atop the majestic peak of Mount Kailash, the stage is set for the celestial union of Lord Shiva and Goddess Parvati. As the supreme ascetic, Shiva resides in deep meditation, surrounded by the ethereal beauty of nature, while Parvati, the embodiment of divine grace and feminine power, seeks to capture his attention through her unwavering devotion.

In this sacred abode, where the veil between the mortal and divine worlds is thinnest, Parvati embarks on a journey of self-discovery and spiritual awakening. Determined to win the heart of Shiva, she undergoes rigorous penance and austerity, immersing herself in the practice of meditation and prayer.

As the days turn into weeks, and the weeks into months, Parvati's devotion knows no bounds. She offers her prayers to Lord Shiva with unwavering faith, her heart filled with love and longing for the divine consort she has yet to meet.

Meanwhile, atop Mount Kailash, Shiva remains absorbed in his meditation, unaffected by the world around him. His divine presence radiates a sense of tranquility and serenity, drawing beings from far and wide to seek his blessings and guidance.

Yet, amidst the celestial splendor of Mount Kailash, there is a sense of longing that pervades the air – a longing for union, for completeness, for the divine dance of Shiva and Parvati to begin.

It is in this backdrop of divine yearning that the paths of Shiva and Parvati converge, setting the stage for a meeting that will forever alter the course of cosmic history.

As the sun sets over the snow-capped peaks of Mount Kailash, casting a golden hue upon the landscape, Parvati prepares herself for her encounter with the supreme ascetic. With her heart brimming with anticipation and her soul ablaze with devotion, she ascends the sacred mountain, her steps guided by an unseen force.

At last, she stands before the meditating form of Lord Shiva, his divine presence casting a spell of awe and reverence upon her. With trembling hands and a voice filled with reverence, she offers her prayers to the Lord of Lords, beseeching him to accept her devotion and grant her the boon of becoming his divine consort.

In that sacred moment, the universe holds its breath as Shiva opens his eyes, his gaze meeting Parvati's with a depth of understanding that transcends words. In that silent exchange, a bond is forged – a bond of love, of destiny, of eternal union.

And thus begins the divine encounter on Mount Kailash, where the cosmic dance of Shiva and Parvati unfolds in all its splendor, weaving together the threads of fate and destiny in a tapestry of divine love and eternal devotion.

The Test of Devotion

As the dawn breaks over the tranquil slopes of Mount Kailash, Parvati's heart is filled with a sense of anticipation and trepidation. She awaits Lord Shiva's response to her fervent prayers, hoping against hope that her devotion has found favor in his eyes.

In the presence of the supreme ascetic, Parvati finds herself consumed by a sense of awe and reverence. His divine aura, radiating with transcendent power, leaves her breathless, her soul stirred by a longing she cannot fully comprehend.

Yet, despite her awe, Parvati remains steadfast in her resolve. With unwavering faith and determination, she continues to offer her prayers to Lord Shiva, her heart overflowing with love and devotion.

But as the days turn into weeks, and still, there is no sign of Shiva's response, doubt begins to creep into Parvati's heart. Has her penance been in vain? Has her love gone unnoticed by the supreme ascetic?

In the depths of her despair, Parvati turns to the sage Narada, the celestial troubadour known for his wisdom and insight. With tears in her eyes, she pours out her heart to the sage, seeking his counsel and guidance in her time of need.

Moved by Parvati's plight, Narada offers her words of solace and encouragement. He assures her that her devotion has not gone unnoticed by Lord Shiva, and that her love will be reciprocated in due time.

Encouraged by Narada's words, Parvati resolves to continue her penance with renewed vigor and determination. With each passing day, her love for Shiva grows stronger, her faith unwavering in the face of adversity.

And then, one fateful day, as Parvati sits in meditation atop Mount Kailash, her prayers are answered in the most unexpected of ways. A divine voice resonates through the heavens, proclaiming that her love and devotion have touched the heart of Lord Shiva, and that he will soon appear before her to grant her boon.

Overwhelmed with joy and gratitude, Parvati's heart soars as she awaits the arrival of her beloved. And as the sun sets over the sacred mountain, casting a golden glow upon the landscape, Lord Shiva appears before her, his divine presence illuminating the heavens with a brilliance that defies description.

In that moment of divine communion, Shiva and Parvati's destinies become intertwined, setting the stage for a love story that will span the ages and inspire generations to come.

Parvati's Tapasya

With the assurance of Lord Shiva's imminent arrival, Parvati's heart is filled with a newfound sense of purpose and determination. She redoubles her efforts in penance, immersing herself in rigorous tapasya (austerity) to prepare herself for the divine union that awaits her.

High atop Mount Kailash, where the air is thin and the elements unforgiving, Parvati embarks on a journey of self-purification and spiritual awakening. She chooses a secluded spot beneath the shade of an ancient banyan tree, where she sits in meditation, her eyes closed in deep concentration.

In the beginning, Parvati finds herself beset by distractions – the howling of the wind, the chatter of birds, the rustling of leaves. But with each passing day, she learns to quiet the noise of the external world and turn her focus inward, to the stillness of her own being.

As the days stretch into weeks, Parvati's tapasya becomes more intense. She subsists on a diet of fruits and roots, eschewing all forms of luxury and comfort. She subjects her body to harsh physical disciplines, performing arduous yogic postures and enduring long hours of meditation.

But it is not only the physical hardships that Parvati must endure; she also faces the challenges of her own mind and emotions. Doubt and fear creep into her thoughts, tempting her to abandon her quest for union with Shiva and return to the comforts of her former life.

Yet, with each passing day, Parvati finds strength in her love for Shiva, drawing courage from the depths of her heart. She reminds herself of the divine purpose that guides her, and she presses onward with renewed determination.

As the days turn into weeks, and the weeks into months, Parvati's tapasya bears fruit. Her soul becomes purified by the fire of her devotion, her mind attuned to the cosmic vibrations of the universe. In moments of deep meditation, she experiences visions of Lord Shiva, his divine form appearing before her like a beacon of light in the darkness.

Overwhelmed with joy and gratitude, Parvati falls to her knees, offering her prayers of thanks to the Lord of Lords. In that moment of divine communion, she knows that her tapasya has not been in vain – that her love and devotion have brought her one step closer to the divine union she seeks.

And so, with her heart filled with hope and anticipation, Parvati continues her tapasya, knowing that soon she will be reunited with her beloved Shiva in a union that will transcend the boundaries of mortal existence.

Shiva's Trials

As Parvati immerses herself in rigorous tapasya atop Mount Kailash, Lord Shiva, the supreme ascetic, remains absorbed in his meditation, unaware of the divine drama unfolding around him. Yet, the cosmic energies of the universe stir, and the wheels of destiny are set into motion, bringing Shiva and Parvati ever closer to their fated union.

For Shiva, the journey towards union with Parvati is not without its trials and tribulations. As the lord of destruction and transformation, he is tasked with maintaining the cosmic balance, and his divine duties often take him far from the tranquil slopes of Mount Kailash.

Throughout the ages, Shiva wanders the length and breadth of the universe, his path fraught with challenges and obstacles. He battles demons and asuras, tames wild forces of nature, and dispenses justice to those who seek to disrupt the harmony of the cosmos.

Yet, amidst the chaos and turmoil of the mortal world, Shiva remains steadfast in his resolve. His heart is untouched by desire, his mind unruffled by the temptations of power and wealth. He is the embodiment of detachment, the eternal witness to the ebb and flow of existence.

But even the great lord of destruction is not immune to the allure of divine love. As the cosmic energies converge to bring Shiva and Parvati together, he feels a stirring in his heart – a longing for union, for companionship, for the divine counterpart who will complete him.

And so, as Parvati's tapasya reaches its zenith, Shiva's thoughts turn to the gentle goddess who sits in meditation atop Mount Kailash. He feels a pull towards her, a magnetic attraction that transcends the boundaries of time and space.

But before Shiva can unite with Parvati, he must undergo a series of trials and tests, designed to purify his soul and prepare him for the divine union that awaits him. These trials take him to the far corners of the universe, where he must confront his inner demons and overcome the obstacles that stand in his path.

Yet, through it all, Shiva remains resolute, his faith unwavering in the face of adversity. He knows that each trial is but a stepping stone on the path towards union with Parvati, and he embraces them with humility and grace.

And so, as the cosmic drama unfolds, Shiva's trials pave the way for the ultimate reunion with his beloved Parvati, setting the stage for a love story that will transcend the boundaries of mortal existence and endure for eternity.

Blessings of the
Divine Beings

As Parvati continues her tapasya atop Mount Kailash and Shiva undergoes his trials across the cosmos, the divine beings of the universe take notice of the unfolding drama. Moved by the purity of Parvati's devotion and the steadfastness of Shiva's resolve, they gather to bestow their blessings upon the divine couple.

High in the heavens, the gods and goddesses assemble in their celestial abodes, their hearts filled with reverence and awe for the love that blossoms between Shiva and Parvati. Lord Brahma, the creator of the cosmos, sits upon his lotus throne, his four faces beaming with divine radiance. He offers his benedictions for the success of Parvati's tapasya and Shiva's trials, his voice resonating with the power of creation itself. With each word, he infuses their beings with the essence of divine love, ensuring that their union will endure for all eternity.

Goddess Lakshmi, the embodiment of wealth and prosperity, stands beside Lord Brahma, her golden form radiant with divine light. She showers Parvati with her blessings, promising her abundance and prosperity in her life with Shiva. With a wave of her hand, she bestows upon them the riches of the universe, ensuring that they will want for nothing in their divine abode.

Lord Vishnu, the preserver of the universe, sits upon his celestial throne, his eyes closed in deep meditation. He offers his protection to Parvati and Shiva as they embark on their journey together, his divine presence pervading the cosmos. With a gentle smile, he assures them that he will watch over them and guide them through the trials and tribulations that lie ahead, ensuring their safety and well-being on their path to union.

The celestial sages and saints also join in the divine chorus, their voices raised in hymns of praise and adoration. They offer their prayers and blessings for the success of Parvati's tapasya and Shiva's trials, invoking the powers of the cosmos to aid the divine couple in their quest for union. With each chant, they send forth waves of divine energy, enveloping Shiva and Parvati in a cocoon of divine protection.

And so, as the blessings of the divine beings rain down upon them, Shiva and Parvati feel their hearts filled with joy and gratitude. They know that they are not alone in their journey, that the gods and goddesses of the universe stand with them, guiding them on the path towards union and eternal bliss.

With renewed determination and faith, Shiva and Parvati continue their respective quests, knowing that they are destined to be together, forever bound by the bonds of love and devotion that transcend the boundaries of time and space.

The Celestial Announcement

As Parvati's tapasya reaches its zenith atop Mount Kailash and Shiva completes his trials across the cosmos, a sense of anticipation grips the celestial realms. The gods and goddesses, along with the celestial beings, eagerly await the divine union of Shiva and Parvati, knowing that their love will bring harmony and balance to the universe.

In the celestial court, Lord Indra, the king of the gods, convenes a grand assembly of divine beings to announce the impending union of Shiva and Parvati. With a thunderous clap of his hands, he calls the gathering to order, his voice resonating with authority and power.

Surrounded by the assembled gods, goddesses, sages, and celestial beings, Lord Indra stands upon his golden throne, his regal form radiating with divine light. He speaks with eloquence and grace, proclaiming the love story of Shiva and Parvati to all who have gathered, his words carrying the weight of destiny.

As Lord Indra recounts the tale of Parvati's tapasya and Shiva's trials, a sense of reverence and awe fills the celestial court. The gods and goddesses listen intently, their hearts filled with admiration for the devotion and steadfastness of the divine couple.

With each word, Lord Indra paints a vivid picture of the love that blossoms between Shiva and Parvati, describing their divine union as a beacon of hope and inspiration for all beings. He speaks of their eternal bond, forged in the fires of devotion and tempered by the trials of fate, and he declares that their love will endure for all eternity.

As the celestial announcement reverberates through the heavens, the celestial beings rejoice, their voices raised in hymns of praise and adoration. They offer their prayers and blessings for the success of Shiva and Parvati's union, knowing that their love will bring peace and prosperity to the universe.

And so, as the celestial announcement draws to a close, the gods and goddesses of the celestial realms bow their heads in reverence, acknowledging the divine plan that unfolds before them. They know that the union of Shiva and Parvati is not only a testament to their love but also a symbol of hope and renewal for all beings.

With hearts filled with joy and anticipation, the celestial beings await the moment when Shiva and Parvati will be reunited, knowing that their love will shine like a beacon of light in the darkness, guiding all beings towards the path of enlightenment and eternal bliss.

Poem; The Love of Shiva and Parvati

In the sacred realm where mountains kiss the sky,
　A love story unfolds, eternal and high.
Shiva, the ascetic, in meditation deep,
Parvati, his beloved, her love to keep.
Atop Mount Kailash, where the heavens meet,
Parvati's devotion, pure and sweet.
Through tapasya and trials, she seeks her Lord,
In silent meditation, her love is poured.
Shiva, the cosmic dancer, with eyes closed tight,
Feels Parvati's love, a beacon of light.
Through realms of time and space, his spirit flies,
Drawn to her devotion, her love that never dies.
In the celestial court, the gods decree,
The union of Shiva and Parvati, pure and free.
Their love, a symphony of cosmic grace,
An eternal dance in the celestial space.
Through trials and tribulations, their love does bloom,
In the divine embrace, there's no sense of gloom.
For in each other's arms, they find their bliss,
A love that transcends, a divine kiss.
Oh, Shiva and Parvati, in love entwined,

A union so sacred, so divinely aligned.
In the dance of creation, their love does sway,
Forever united, in eternal play.
So let us sing the praises of love divine,
Of Shiva and Parvati, whose hearts entwine.
In their eternal embrace, may we find,
The true essence of love, pure and kind.

Trials and Tribulations

The Cosmic Challenges

In the vast expanse of the cosmos, where stars twinkle and galaxies swirl in a dance of cosmic wonder, Shiva embarks on a journey fraught with trials and tribulations. As the lord of destruction and transformation, his path is not one of ease, but of challenges that test his resolve and shape his destiny.

The first trial that confronts Shiva is that of the demon horde, led by the fearsome Raktabija. With their dark powers and malevolent intentions, they seek to disrupt the balance of the universe and plunge it into chaos. But Shiva, with his unwavering courage and divine prowess, confronts the demons head-on, his third eye blazing with righteous fury.

In a cosmic battle that spans the heavens and the earth, Shiva battles the demon horde with a ferocity that shakes the very foundations of the universe. With each blow of his trident, he strikes fear into the hearts of his enemies, his divine form radiating with the power of a thousand suns.

But the trials do not end there, for Shiva must also face the challenges of his own inner demons. As the lord of destruction, he is tasked with maintaining the balance between creation and dissolution, a burden that weighs heavily upon his soul. In moments of doubt and despair, he questions his own divine purpose, wondering if his actions serve the greater good or merely perpetuate the cycle of suffering.

Yet, through it all, Shiva remains steadfast in his resolve, his faith unwavering in the face of adversity. With each trial he faces, he grows stronger and more resolute, his spirit tempered by the fires of divine grace.

And so, as Shiva continues his journey through the cosmos, he knows that the trials and tribulations he faces are but stepping stones on the path towards enlightenment. For in the crucible of adversity, he discovers the true essence of his being – a being of infinite love, compassion, and divine grace.

As the stars twinkle in the velvet sky and the galaxies swirl in a dance of cosmic wonder, Shiva's journey continues, guided by the light of his own divine essence. And though the trials may be many and the challenges great, he knows that with each step he takes, he draws closer to the ultimate truth – the truth of his own divine nature and the eternal love that binds all beings in the embrace of cosmic grace.

The Test of Faith

As Shiva journeys through the cosmos, he encounters a series of trials that test not only his physical prowess but also his faith in the cosmic order. Among the myriad challenges he faces, one of the most profound is the test of faith – a trial that forces him to confront the depths of his own belief and trust in the divine plan.

In the heart of a distant galaxy, Shiva finds himself confronted by a cosmic void, a vast expanse of darkness that threatens to engulf him in its depths. With each step he takes, the void seems to grow larger, its darkness more suffocating, its emptiness more profound.

Yet, in the face of this existential challenge, Shiva draws upon the strength of his faith, knowing that the light of divine grace shines even in the darkest of times. With unwavering determination, he presses onward, his heart filled with the knowledge that he is guided by the hand of destiny.

As he traverses the cosmic void, Shiva encounters beings of darkness and despair, entities that seek to extinguish the light of his spirit and drag him into the abyss of oblivion. But with each encounter, he stands firm in his conviction, his faith shining like a beacon of hope in the darkness.

In moments of doubt and uncertainty, Shiva calls upon the wisdom of the ancient sages and saints, drawing inspiration from their teachings and guidance. Through their words of wisdom, he finds strength in the knowledge that the trials he faces are but illusions of the mind, manifestations of the ego's resistance to the divine will.

And so, with each step he takes, Shiva learns to surrender more fully to the flow of cosmic grace, knowing that the universe is always guiding him towards his ultimate destiny. In the crucible of the cosmic void, he discovers the true essence of faith – a faith that transcends all doubt and fear, a faith that is rooted in the eternal truth of his own divine nature.

As Shiva emerges from the depths of the cosmic void, his faith stronger than ever, he knows that he has passed the test of faith with flying colors. With renewed determination, he continues his journey through the cosmos, knowing that whatever trials may lie ahead, he will face them with the unwavering faith of a true devotee of the divine.

The Temptation of Desire

As Shiva's cosmic journey unfolds, he finds himself confronted by yet another trial - the temptation of desire. In the midst of his quest for enlightenment, he encounters beings of exquisite beauty and allure, whose seductive charms threaten to lead him astray from the path of righteousness.

In a celestial realm bathed in the golden light of a thousand suns, Shiva encounters the divine nymphs known as the Apsaras. With their graceful movements and enchanting melodies, they dance before him, their beauty rivaling that of the celestial gods themselves.

Entranced by their ethereal beauty, Shiva feels a stirring in his heart – a longing that threatens to consume him with desire. For a fleeting moment, he is tempted to abandon his quest for enlightenment and lose himself in the embrace of the divine nymphs.

But even as desire threatens to overwhelm him, Shiva draws upon the strength of his inner resolve, knowing that the path to true liberation lies not in the indulgence of worldly pleasures, but in the renunciation of desire itself. With a resolute heart, he resists the temptation of the Apsaras, his mind focused firmly on the pursuit of spiritual truth.

As he turns away from the seductive allure of the divine nymphs, Shiva is met with yet another test of his resolve. This time, it is the temptation of power and glory, as he encounters beings of immense strength and prowess who offer him dominion over the cosmos in exchange for his allegiance.

But Shiva, ever mindful of the transient nature of power and fame, rejects their offer without hesitation, knowing that true greatness lies not in the accumulation of worldly possessions, but in the cultivation of inner virtue and wisdom.

And so, with each temptation he faces, Shiva emerges stronger and more resolute, his spirit unshaken by the trials of the material world. For he knows that the path to enlightenment is not an easy one, but one that requires unwavering determination and steadfast devotion to the divine.

As he continues his cosmic journey, Shiva remains ever vigilant, knowing that the temptations of desire and power will always lurk on the fringes of his consciousness, waiting to test his resolve. But with the grace of the divine guiding him, he is confident that he will emerge victorious, his spirit purified by the fires of adversity and his heart filled with the eternal light of truth.

The Ordeal of Separation

As Shiva's cosmic journey progresses, he finds himself confronted by an ordeal that strikes at the very core of his being – the ordeal of separation. For amidst the vastness of the cosmos, he is separated from his beloved Parvati, the goddess whose love sustains him through the trials and tribulations of his quest.

In the depths of his heart, Shiva feels a longing – a yearning for the presence of his beloved, whose divine essence fills his soul with boundless joy and light. Yet, no matter how far he searches, he cannot find her, for she exists in a realm beyond the reach of mortal eyes.

With each passing moment of separation, Shiva feels the weight of loneliness pressing down upon him, his heart heavy with the ache of longing. For Parvati is not merely his consort, but his soulmate, the one who completes him in every way.

As he wanders through the vast expanse of the cosmos, Shiva is haunted by visions of his beloved, her radiant form shimmering like a mirage in the desert of his soul. In moments of despair, he calls out her name, his voice echoing through the empty void of space, but she remains elusive, a distant dream that fades with the light of dawn.

Yet, even in the depths of his despair, Shiva draws strength from the memory of Parvati's love, knowing that she is with him always, guiding him on his journey through the cosmos. With each step he takes, he feels her presence beside him, her love a beacon of light in the darkness of his solitude.

In moments of quiet reflection, Shiva closes his eyes and meditates upon the divine form of Parvati, her beauty shining like a thousand suns in the depths of his consciousness. In these moments of communion, he feels their souls merge as one, transcending the boundaries of time and space to dwell in the eternal realm of love.

And so, even as he grapples with the pain of separation, Shiva remains steadfast in his devotion to Parvati, knowing that their love will endure for all eternity. For theirs is a love that transcends the limitations of mortal existence, a love that is as boundless as the cosmos itself.

The Quest for Reunion

As Shiva navigates the cosmic expanse, his longing for Parvati grows stronger with each passing moment of separation. Determined to reunite with his beloved, he embarks on a quest that will test his courage, resilience, and unwavering devotion.

With the fire of determination burning in his heart, Shiva searches every corner of the universe, his eyes scanning the celestial realms for any sign of Parvati's divine presence. He traverses the galaxies, journeys through the star-strewn skies, and delves into the depths of the cosmic ocean, his spirit undaunted by the vastness of the task before him.

Along the way, Shiva encounters beings of light and darkness, each offering clues and guidance to aid him in his quest. He listens to the whispers of the cosmic winds, reads the signs written in the constellations, and follows the path illuminated by the light of his own inner knowing.

Through trials and tribulations, Shiva's determination never wavers, his love for Parvati driving him ever onward. He faces challenges that test his strength and resolve, battles demons that seek to thwart his quest, and overcomes obstacles that stand in the way of his reunion with his beloved.

Yet, amidst the chaos and turmoil of his journey, Shiva finds moments of peace and clarity, moments when the veil of illusion is lifted and he glimpses the eternal truth that lies beyond. In these moments of divine communion, he feels Parvati's presence beside him, her love guiding him like a beacon of light in the darkness.

And so, with each step he takes, Shiva draws closer to his beloved, his heart filled with hope and anticipation. For he knows that no matter how arduous the journey may be, no matter how many obstacles lie in his path, he will find his way back to Parvati's loving embrace.

And as the cosmic dance of creation unfolds around him, Shiva presses onward, his soul aflame with the fire of divine love. For he knows that the quest for reunion is not merely a journey of the body, but a journey of the soul – a journey that will lead him back to the eternal embrace of his beloved Parvati.

The Union of Souls

After what feels like an eternity of searching and longing, Shiva's quest for reunion with Parvati reaches its culmination. In the heart of the cosmic expanse, amidst the swirling nebulae and shimmering stars, the divine lovers are finally reunited, their souls merging in a timeless embrace.

As Shiva beholds Parvati's radiant form, his heart swells with overwhelming joy and gratitude. He reaches out to her, his hands trembling with emotion, and she meets him halfway, her eyes shining with love and devotion. In that sacred moment, time stands still, and the universe holds its breath as the two souls become one.

In the celestial realms, the gods and goddesses look on with awe and reverence, their hearts filled with joy at the sight of Shiva and Parvati's divine union. For they know that in the embrace of their love, all is right in the cosmos, and harmony is restored to the universe once more.

As Shiva and Parvati bask in the radiance of their love, they are surrounded by a chorus of celestial beings, whose voices rise in song and celebration. The heavens resound with the music of the spheres, as the stars themselves join in the celestial dance of joy.

In that moment of divine communion, Shiva and Parvati transcend the limitations of mortal existence, their love transcending time and space to dwell in the eternal realm of the soul. For theirs is a love that knows no bounds, a love that is as boundless as the cosmos itself.

And so, as the cosmic dance of creation continues to unfold around them, Shiva and Parvati stand united in their love, their souls entwined for all eternity. In the embrace of their union, they find the ultimate fulfillment – the fulfillment of divine love, pure and true.

And as the stars twinkle in the velvet sky and the galaxies swirl in a dance of cosmic wonder, Shiva and Parvati's love shines like a beacon of light in the darkness, guiding all beings towards the path of enlightenment and eternal bliss.

Poem; Eternal Union: The Love of Shiva and Parvati

In the cosmic dance where stars collide,
    Two souls entwined, side by side.
Shiva, the lord of cosmic might,
Parvati, his beloved, shining bright.
Through trials and tribulations they've faced,
Their love enduring, never displaced.
In the depths of the universe, they sought,
For the eternal bond they both had wrought.
With each trial, their love grew strong,
A union eternal, a cosmic song.
Through the void of separation's pain,
Their hearts connected, love to sustain.
In the dance of creation, they found,
A love profound, forever bound.
With eyes that sparkled like the night,
And hearts that beat with pure delight.
In the union of their souls, they found,
The true essence of love, unbound.
For in each other's arms, they knew,

That love eternal, forever true.
So let the stars in the heavens above,
Bear witness to their eternal love.
For in the cosmic dance, they'll remain,
Shiva and Parvati, forever the same.

Divine Interventions

The Hand of Destiny

In the grand tapestry of existence, there are moments when the hand of destiny reaches down from the heavens to shape the course of mortal lives. Such is the case with the divine interventions that unfold in the timeless love story of Shiva and Parvati, where the gods and goddesses of the cosmos play an integral role in guiding the path of the divine couple.

At the heart of these interventions lies the celestial council, where the gods and goddesses convene to discuss the unfolding drama of Shiva and Parvati's love. Led by Lord Brahma, the creator of the universe, and attended by the divine beings of the cosmos, the council deliberates on the fates of the divine couple, weaving together the threads of destiny with divine wisdom and grace.

It is in these sacred chambers that the course of Shiva and Parvati's love is shaped, as the gods and goddesses conspire to bring them together in divine union. Through their interventions, they orchestrate the events that will lead the divine couple towards their ultimate destiny, ensuring that love will triumph over all obstacles.

One such intervention comes in the form of divine signs and omens, which appear to Shiva and Parvati as they embark on their respective quests. These signs serve as guiding lights, leading them ever closer to one another and affirming the eternal bond that binds their souls together.

Another intervention takes the form of celestial messengers, who are dispatched by the gods to aid Shiva and Parvati in their trials and tribulations. These messengers offer words of wisdom and encouragement, guiding the divine couple through the darkest moments of their journey and reminding them of the divine plan that unfolds before them.

Yet perhaps the most profound intervention of all is the divine grace that permeates every moment of Shiva and Parvati's love story. It is this grace that sustains them through the trials of separation and strengthens their resolve in the face of adversity. It is this grace that ultimately leads them back to one another, ensuring that their love will endure for all eternity.

And so, as the gods and goddesses of the celestial council continue to weave the threads of destiny, Shiva and Parvati move ever closer towards their divine union, guided by the hand of destiny and the eternal light of love.

The Blessings of the Celestial Beings

As Shiva and Parvati journey towards their destined union, they are showered with the blessings of the celestial beings who watch over them with benevolent eyes. From the highest realms of the cosmos to the deepest depths of the earth, the divine couple is surrounded by a chorus of celestial voices, guiding them on their path of love and devotion.

High atop Mount Kailash, where Shiva resides in solitary meditation, the celestial beings gather to offer their blessings to the divine couple. Lord Brahma, with his four faces shining with divine radiance, bestows upon them the boon of eternal love and union, ensuring that their bond will endure for all eternity.

Goddess Lakshmi, the embodiment of beauty and grace, showers Parvati with her blessings, adorning her with jewels and blessings of prosperity. She promises to watch over the divine couple and blesses their union with abundance and happiness, ensuring that they will want for nothing in their divine abode.

Lord Vishnu, the preserver of the universe, stands beside Lord Brahma, his eyes filled with compassion and wisdom. He offers his protection to Shiva and Parvati, promising to guide them through the trials and tribulations that lie ahead, ensuring their safety and well-being on their journey towards union.

The celestial sages and saints also join in the chorus of blessings, their voices raised in hymns of praise and adoration. They offer their prayers for the success of Shiva and Parvati's union, invoking the powers of the cosmos to aid them in their quest for love and enlightenment.

And so, as the blessings of the celestial beings rain down upon them, Shiva and Parvati feel their hearts filled with gratitude and joy. They know that they are not alone in their journey, that the gods and goddesses of the cosmos stand with them, guiding them on the path towards eternal love and union.

With renewed determination and faith, Shiva and Parvati continue their journey, knowing that they are destined to be together, forever bound by the blessings of the celestial beings and the eternal light of love that shines within their hearts.

The Guidance of the Divine Signs

As Shiva and Parvati navigate the twists and turns of their divine journey, they are guided by the subtle yet powerful influence of divine signs that manifest in the world around them. These signs, sent forth by the gods and goddesses of the cosmos, serve as beacons of guidance, illuminating the path of the divine couple and reaffirming their destined union.

In the sacred groves of Mount Kailash, where Shiva dwells in solitary meditation, the natural world itself becomes a canvas upon which the divine signs are painted. From the whispering of the wind to the rustling of the leaves, every aspect of nature sings the praises of Shiva and Parvati's love, reminding them of the eternal bond that binds their souls together.

In the celestial realms, the stars themselves align to form patterns and constellations that offer guidance to the divine couple. From the twinkling of the North Star to the dance of the Pleiades, each celestial formation holds a message of hope and encouragement, guiding Shiva and Parvati on their path towards union.

But perhaps the most profound of all divine signs is the silent language of the heart, which speaks to Shiva and Parvati in moments of quiet reflection and meditation. In the depths of their souls, they feel the gentle whisperings of divine guidance, urging them onward in their quest for love and enlightenment.

With each divine sign they encounter, Shiva and Parvati feel their spirits lifted and their resolve strengthened. They know that they are not alone in their journey, but are guided by the hand of destiny and the eternal wisdom of the cosmos.

And so, as they continue on their path, Shiva and Parvati remain ever vigilant for the signs that will lead them towards their destined union. For they know that in the language of the divine, every sign is a message of love and grace, guiding them towards the fulfillment of their divine purpose.

The Guardians of Fate

In the celestial realm where the threads of destiny are woven, there exist guardians who watch over the lives of mortals and shape the course of their destinies. These guardians, entrusted with the sacred task of guiding the souls of the cosmos, play a pivotal role in the love story of Shiva and Parvati, ensuring that their union unfolds according to the divine plan.

Among these guardians is Lord Ganesha, the beloved son of Shiva and Parvati, whose divine presence illuminates their path with wisdom and grace. As the remover of obstacles, Lord Ganesha clears away the barriers that stand between Shiva and Parvati, paving the way for their destined union with his divine blessings.

Another guardian of fate is Lord Kartikeya, the valiant warrior who leads the celestial armies into battle against the forces of darkness. With his indomitable spirit and unwavering courage, Lord Kartikeya stands as a stalwart defender of Shiva and Parvati, ensuring that their love remains unchallenged by the trials of the material world.

But perhaps the most mysterious of all guardians is Nandi, the divine bull who serves as the mount of Lord Shiva. With his keen intuition and unwavering loyalty, Nandi guides Shiva and Parvati through the labyrinthine paths of destiny, leading them ever closer towards their destined union with his silent wisdom.

As Shiva and Parvati navigate the twists and turns of their cosmic journey, they are guided and protected by these guardians of fate, whose divine presence surrounds them like a cloak of celestial light. With each step they take, they feel the reassuring presence of these divine beings by their side, guiding them towards the fulfillment of their divine purpose.

And so, as Shiva and Parvati's love story unfolds amidst the cosmic dance of creation, they remain ever grateful for the guidance and protection of the guardians of fate, knowing that their love is blessed by the divine and destined to endure for all eternity.

The Intercession of Divine Messengers

In the celestial expanse where the tapestry of fate is woven, divine messengers emerge as celestial conduits, bridging the realms of mortals and immortals. These ethereal emissaries, enveloped in the radiance of divine wisdom, emerge to offer solace and guidance to Shiva and Parvati, guiding them through the labyrinth of destiny towards their destined union.

Among these celestial envoys is Lord Vishnu, the benevolent preserver of the cosmos, who descends from his celestial abode to lend his omniscient gaze to the journey of Shiva and Parvati. With his divine presence illuminating their path, he becomes their celestial guide, steering them through the intricacies of cosmic destiny, ensuring that their love remains steadfast amidst the trials of mortal existence.

Goddess Saraswati, the epitome of wisdom and enlightenment, also graces the divine couple with her celestial radiance. Her ethereal presence infuses their journey with the light of knowledge, empowering them to transcend the limitations of mortal understanding and grasp the profound truths that lie at the heart of their divine union.

Lord Indra, the resplendent king of the heavens, rallies the celestial forces to safeguard Shiva and Parvati from the malevolent forces that seek to disrupt their sacred union. With his thunderous voice and unwavering resolve, he stands as their stalwart protector, ensuring that their love remains unscathed by the forces of chaos and destruction that threaten to engulf the cosmos.

As Shiva and Parvati traverse the celestial realms, they are enveloped in a symphony of celestial voices, each resounding with the harmonious melodies of divine guidance and protection. With each step they take, they feel the comforting embrace of these celestial beings, their presence serving as a beacon of hope and assurance amidst the tumultuous currents of cosmic destiny.

And so, as Shiva and Parvati's divine odyssey unfolds amidst the celestial tapestry of creation, they remain ever grateful for the intercession of the divine messengers, whose benevolent guidance and protection pave the way for the fulfillment of their eternal love.

The Convergence of Cosmic Forces

In the grand orchestration of cosmic energies, there unfolds a magnificent convergence that orchestrates the destiny of Shiva and Parvati with celestial precision. Amidst the vast expanse of the celestial realms, where stars twinkle in unison and galaxies spiral in cosmic dance, the divine couple becomes ensconced in the embrace of divine forces, propelling them inexorably towards their fated union.

At the nucleus of this cosmic convergence lies the intricate interplay of celestial bodies – the planets, stars, and galaxies – whose celestial dance mirrors the eternal union of Shiva and Parvati. With each celestial body in perfect alignment, the cosmic symphony resonates with the harmonious vibrations of divine love, guiding the divine couple along the path of their destined reunion.

As Shiva and Parvati traverse the celestial expanse, they become attuned to the subtle pulsations of cosmic energy that permeate the fabric of the universe. They feel the gentle tug of celestial forces, like invisible threads woven by the hand of destiny, drawing them ever closer towards one another with each passing moment.

Amidst the cosmic convergence, a chorus of celestial beings emerges, their voices harmonizing in a celestial symphony that reverberates throughout the cosmos. From the celestial sages and saints who offer prayers of divine benediction to the celestial nymphs and deities who bestow their blessings upon the divine couple, every denizen of the celestial realms joins in the celestial chorus, showering Shiva and Parvati with celestial grace and favor.

In this sublime moment of cosmic convergence, Shiva and Parvati feel the transcendent energies of the universe coursing through their beings, uniting them in a sacred bond that transcends the limitations of mortal existence. They stand at the nexus of creation, surrounded by the eternal dance of cosmic forces that shape the destiny of all beings.

And so, as Shiva and Parvati stand on the threshold of their destined union, they embrace the celestial energies that envelop them, knowing that they are but instruments in the grand cosmic symphony of life, guided by the hand of destiny and the eternal light of love that burns within their hearts.

Poem; Cosmic Embrace

In the celestial expanse where stars doth dance,
    Two souls entwined in divine romance.
Shiva, the lord of cosmic might,
Parvati, his beloved, shining bright.
Through realms of light and galaxies untold,
Their love unfolds, a tale of old.
In cosmic whispers, their hearts converse,
Bound by love's eternal, celestial verse.
Amidst the cosmic symphony's grand embrace,
Shiva and Parvati find their sacred space.
With every twinkle of a distant star,
Their love transcends, near and far.
In the celestial dance, they find their song,
A love that's steadfast, pure, and strong.
Through trials and tribulations, they endure,
Their love a beacon, forever pure.
In the cosmic tapestry, they find their place,
Two souls entwined in love's embrace.
For in the vast expanse of time and space,
Their love shines bright, a guiding grace.
So let the stars in the heavens above,

Bear witness to their eternal love.
For in the cosmic dance, they'll remain,
Shiva and Parvati, forever the same.

Sacred Bond

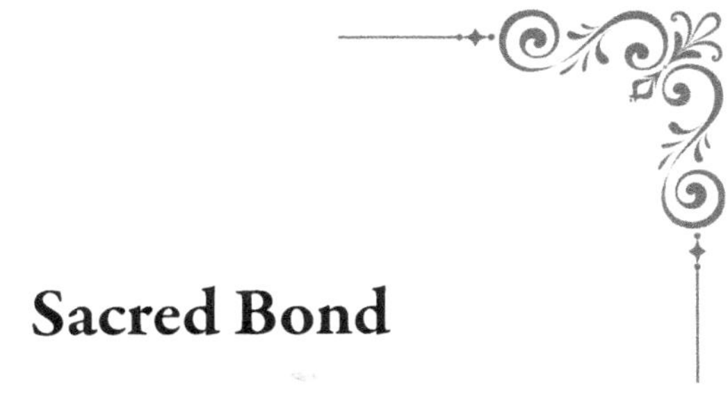

The Cosmic Union

In the boundless expanse of the cosmos, amidst the celestial symphony of stars and galaxies, there exists a sacred bond that transcends the very fabric of existence – the eternal union of Shiva and Parvati. Their love, woven into the tapestry of time itself, stands as a testament to the power of divine connection and the eternal dance of cosmic forces.

At the heart of this sacred bond lies the cosmic union of Shiva, the supreme lord of creation and destruction, and Parvati, the divine embodiment of beauty and grace. From the moment their souls first intertwined amidst the swirling mists of creation, their love has burned brightly, illuminating the darkest corners of the universe with its radiant glow.

Their union is not merely a joining of two souls, but a merging of cosmic energies that reverberate throughout the cosmos, shaping the very essence of existence. With each embrace, each tender caress, Shiva and Parvati weave a tapestry of divine love that spans the breadth of eternity, binding them together in a bond that transcends the limitations of mortal understanding.

As they traverse the celestial realms hand in hand, Shiva and Parvati embody the essence of divine union – a union that is as timeless as the stars themselves, as boundless as the heavens above. Their love knows no bounds, no limitations, for it is a love that exists beyond the realm of mortal comprehension, a love that is as vast and infinite as the cosmos itself.

In the cosmic dance of creation, Shiva and Parvati stand as eternal partners, their souls entwined in a dance of divine ecstasy that echoes throughout the universe. With each step they take, each glance they share, they affirm the eternal nature of their bond, knowing that their love will endure for all eternity, a beacon of light in the infinite expanse of time and space.

And so, as Shiva and Parvati bask in the radiance of their divine union, they embody the eternal truth that love is the very essence of existence, the driving force behind the cosmic dance of creation. For theirs is a love that transcends the boundaries of mortal existence, a love that is as eternal as the stars themselves.

The Celestial Union

In the celestial realm where time is but a fleeting whisper and space an endless expanse, the sacred bond between Shiva and Parvati blossoms into a celestial union that echoes throughout the cosmos. Their love, born of the primordial dance of creation, transcends the confines of mortal existence, weaving together the threads of destiny with the ethereal strands of divine connection.

As they stand amidst the celestial splendor of Mount Kailash, the sacred abode of Lord Shiva, Shiva and Parvati become enveloped in the radiant embrace of their union. With each gaze exchanged, each touch shared, they ignite the heavens with the fire of their love, illuminating the darkest corners of the universe with their divine light.

Their union is not merely a joining of two beings, but a merging of cosmic energies that reverberate throughout the cosmos, shaping the very fabric of existence. From the celestial realms to the farthest reaches of the universe, the echoes of their love resound like celestial melodies, filling the cosmos with the harmonious vibrations of divine union.

As they embark on their cosmic journey together, Shiva and Parvati become the embodiment of divine partnership – a partnership that transcends the boundaries of time and space, uniting them in a bond that is as eternal as the stars themselves. With each step they take, each moment they share, they affirm the eternal nature of their love, knowing that their union is ordained by the hand of destiny itself.

In the celestial dance of creation, Shiva and Parvati become the focal point of divine harmony, their souls entwined in a dance of cosmic ecstasy that resonates throughout the universe. With each movement, each gesture, they affirm the eternal truth that love is the very essence of existence, the driving force behind the cosmic symphony of life.

And so, as Shiva and Parvati's celestial union unfolds amidst the grandeur of the cosmos, they stand as a beacon of light in the infinite expanse of time and space, illuminating the heavens with the radiance of their love. For theirs is a bond that transcends the boundaries of mortal understanding, a bond that is as eternal as the universe itself.

The Cosmic Harmony

In the celestial tapestry woven by the hands of destiny, Shiva and Parvati's sacred bond resonates as a symphony of cosmic harmony, echoing throughout the vast expanse of the universe. Their union, forged in the fires of divine love, serves as a beacon of light in the darkness, guiding all beings towards the path of enlightenment and eternal bliss.

As they traverse the celestial realms hand in hand, Shiva and Parvati become attuned to the subtle rhythms of the cosmos, feeling the pulsations of cosmic energy that flow through their beings. With each breath they take, each heartbeat that echoes in unison, they become one with the cosmic symphony, their souls merging in a divine dance of cosmic harmony.

Their love is not bound by the constraints of time or space, but transcends the very essence of existence itself. In their union, the boundaries between mortal and immortal, finite and infinite, dissolve into the eternal expanse of divine love, where all is one and one is all.

As they gaze upon the celestial wonders that adorn the heavens, Shiva and Parvati find solace in the timeless beauty of the universe, knowing that their love is but a reflection of the eternal dance of creation. With each star that twinkles in the night sky, each planet that orbits its sun, they see the hand of destiny guiding their path, leading them towards the fulfillment of their divine purpose.

In the cosmic dance of creation, Shiva and Parvati become the embodiment of divine harmony, their souls entwined in a celestial embrace that transcends the limitations of mortal understanding. With each moment they share, each word they speak, they affirm the eternal truth that love is the very essence of existence, the cosmic force that binds all beings together in a web of divine connection.

And so, as Shiva and Parvati's sacred bond continues to resonate throughout the cosmos, they stand as eternal witnesses to the cosmic symphony of life, their love serving as a guiding light for all beings on the journey towards enlightenment and eternal bliss.

The Eternal Embrace

In the ethereal realm where the boundaries of time and space dissolve into the cosmic expanse, Shiva and Parvati find themselves engulfed in the eternal embrace of their divine union. At the pinnacle of Mount Kailash, amidst the celestial splendor of the heavens, they stand as the epitome of divine love, their souls intertwined in a dance of cosmic ecstasy that echoes throughout the universe.

Their union is not merely a joining of two beings, but a merging of cosmic energies that resonates with the very essence of existence itself. From the depths of the primordial void to the farthest reaches of the cosmos, the echoes of their love reverberate like celestial melodies, filling the universe with the harmonious vibrations of divine union.

As they stand hand in hand, bathed in the radiant glow of their love, Shiva and Parvati become attuned to the subtle rhythms of the cosmos that flow through their beings. With each breath they take, each heartbeat that echoes in unison, they become one with the cosmic symphony, their souls merging in a divine dance of cosmic harmony.

In the depths of their gaze, the universe finds solace, as Shiva and Parvati become the embodiment of divine partnership – a partnership that transcends the boundaries of time and space, uniting them in a bond that is as eternal as the stars themselves. With each moment they share, each breath they take, they affirm the eternal nature of their love, knowing that their union is ordained by the hand of destiny itself.

Their love is a cosmic phenomenon, a radiant beacon of light that illuminates the heavens with its celestial glow. From the celestial realms to the mortal plane, their love shines forth like a guiding star, leading all beings towards the path of enlightenment and eternal bliss.

Amidst the celestial splendor of Mount Kailash, Shiva and Parvati become the focal point of divine harmony, their souls entwined in a dance of cosmic ecstasy that transcends mortal understanding. With each movement, each gesture, they affirm the eternal truth that love is the very essence of existence, the cosmic force that binds all beings together in a web of divine connection.

In the depths of their love, the mysteries of the universe unfold, as Shiva and Parvati become the custodians of cosmic wisdom and divine knowledge. With each moment they spend together, they unlock the secrets of creation, unraveling the mysteries of the cosmos with their boundless love and infinite understanding.

And so, as Shiva and Parvati's sacred bond continues to resonate throughout the cosmos, they stand as eternal witnesses to the cosmic symphony of life, their love serving as a guiding light for all beings on the journey towards enlightenment and eternal bliss.

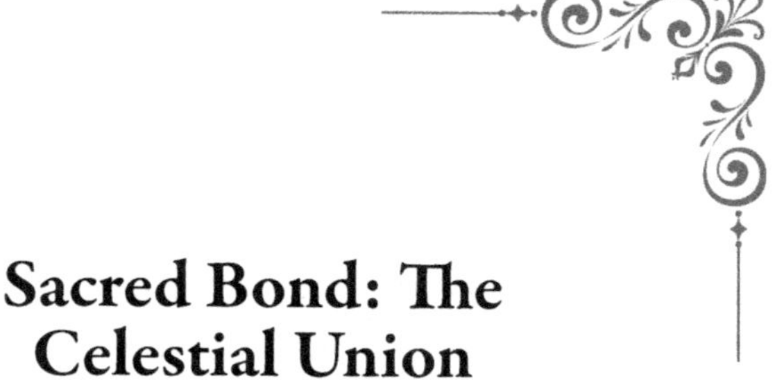

Sacred Bond: The Celestial Union

In the celestial realm, where time dances to the rhythm of eternity and space stretches infinitely, Shiva and Parvati's sacred bond blooms into a celestial union that echoes throughout the cosmos. Their love, born from the very essence of creation, transcends the limitations of mortal existence, intertwining their souls in an eternal dance of cosmic harmony.

As they stand amidst the resplendent beauty of Mount Kailash, the celestial abode of Lord Shiva, Shiva and Parvati find themselves enveloped in the timeless embrace of their union. Each glance exchanged, each touch shared, ignites the heavens with the fiery passion of their love, illuminating the darkest corners of the universe with its radiant glow.

Their union is not merely a convergence of two beings, but a fusion of celestial energies that resonate with the very fabric of existence. From the celestial realms to the furthest reaches of the cosmos, the echoes of their love reverberate like celestial melodies, infusing the universe with the harmonious vibrations of divine union.

In the depth of their connection, the universe finds solace, as Shiva and Parvati become the embodiment of divine partnership – a partnership that transcends the confines of time and space, uniting them in a bond that is as eternal as the cosmos itself. With each moment they share, each breath they take, they reaffirm the timeless nature of their love, knowing that their union is ordained by the hand of destiny.

Their love is a beacon of light in the cosmic expanse, illuminating the heavens with the radiance of its brilliance. From the celestial realms to the mortal plane, their union shines like a guiding star, leading all beings towards the path of enlightenment and eternal bliss.

In the celestial dance of creation, Shiva and Parvati become the focal point of divine harmony, their souls entwined in a cosmic embrace that transcends mortal comprehension. With each movement, each gesture, they affirm the eternal truth that love is the very essence of existence, the cosmic force that binds all beings together in a web of divine connection.

In the depths of their love, the mysteries of the universe unfold, as Shiva and Parvati become the custodians of cosmic wisdom and divine knowledge. With each moment they spend together, they unravel the secrets of creation, unlocking the mysteries of the cosmos with their boundless love and infinite understanding.

And so, as Shiva and Parvati's celestial union continues to resonate throughout the cosmos, they stand as eternal witnesses to the cosmic symphony of life, their love serving as a guiding light for all beings on the journey towards enlightenment and eternal bliss.

The Cosmic Legacy

In the vast expanse of the celestial realm, Shiva and Parvati's sacred bond transcends the boundaries of time and space, leaving an indelible mark on the fabric of existence itself. As they stand united atop Mount Kailash, the cosmic energies of their love intertwine, weaving a tapestry of divine connection that spans the breadth of eternity.

Their union is a testament to the power of love, a force that shapes the destiny of the cosmos and guides the souls of all beings towards enlightenment and eternal bliss. From the celestial realms to the mortal plane, the echoes of their love resound like celestial melodies, inspiring all who hear them to embrace the divine within themselves.

As they gaze upon the celestial wonders that adorn the heavens, Shiva and Parvati find solace in the knowledge that their love is eternal, a guiding light in the infinite expanse of time and space. With each moment they share, each breath they take, they affirm the eternal nature of their bond, knowing that their union is ordained by the hand of destiny itself.

Their love is a beacon of hope in the darkness, illuminating the path of all who seek enlightenment and divine grace. From the celestial sages and saints who offer prayers of benediction to the mortal beings who look to the heavens for guidance, all find solace in the radiant glow of Shiva and Parvati's love.

In the celestial dance of creation, Shiva and Parvati become the embodiment of divine harmony, their souls entwined in a cosmic embrace that transcends mortal understanding. With each movement, each gesture, they affirm the eternal truth that love is the very essence of existence, the cosmic force that binds all beings together in a web of divine connection.

In the depths of their love, the mysteries of the universe unfold, as Shiva and Parvati become the custodians of cosmic wisdom and divine knowledge. With each moment they spend together, they unlock the secrets of creation, guiding all beings towards enlightenment and eternal bliss.

And so, as Shiva and Parvati's cosmic legacy continues to resonate throughout the cosmos, they stand as eternal witnesses to the cosmic symphony of life, their love serving as a guiding light for all beings on the journey towards enlightenment and eternal bliss.

Poem; Eternal Embrace: Shiva and Parvati

In realms where stars whisper secrets untold,
Two souls entwine, their love unfolds.
Shiva, the lord of cosmic might,
Parvati, his beloved, shining bright.
Amidst celestial splendor, their bond aglow,
Infinite love, like rivers that flow.
Their union transcends mortal plight,
In the cosmic dance, their spirits ignite.
Mount Kailash, their celestial throne,
Infinite love, to them is known.
With each embrace, the heavens ignite,
Their love, a beacon in the cosmic night.
In the depths of space, their whispers heard,
A symphony of love, like a sacred word.
Infinite cosmos, their souls entwine,
In eternal embrace, their destinies align.
Their love, a cosmic dance unfurled,
Echoes of eternity, in every world.
In celestial realms, their legacy told,

Eternal embrace, a love to behold.

Epic Journeys

The Call to Adventure

In the annals of cosmic history, amidst the swirling nebulae and celestial wonders, lies the tale of Shiva and Parvati's epic journey - a saga woven with threads of destiny and woven with the fabric of the cosmos itself. Theirs is a journey that spans the expanse of time and space, a quest born of love and illuminated by divine purpose.

It begins with the call to adventure, a whisper carried on the cosmic winds that stirs the hearts of gods and mortals alike. For Shiva, the great ascetic and lord of destruction, it is a call that beckons him to seek his divine counterpart, Parvati, the embodiment of beauty and grace. And for Parvati, it is a call that awakens within her the longing to unite with her beloved, Shiva, and fulfill their sacred destiny.

Guided by the hand of destiny, Shiva and Parvati embark on their epic journey, leaving behind the celestial realms and venturing into the unknown depths of the universe. Along the way, they encounter celestial beings and divine messengers who offer guidance and wisdom, aiding them on their quest to unite their souls in eternal love.

But their journey is not without challenges, for the cosmic forces of creation and destruction conspire to test their resolve and challenge their devotion. From the treacherous paths of the celestial mountains to the depths of the cosmic oceans, Shiva and Parvati face trials and tribulations that threaten to tear them apart.

Yet, with each obstacle they overcome, their love grows stronger, their bond forged in the fires of adversity and tempered by the trials of their epic journey. For Shiva and Parvati, the call to adventure is not just a quest for love, but a journey of self-discovery and enlightenment, a path that leads them towards the realization of their divine purpose.

And so, as Shiva and Parvati's epic journey unfolds amidst the cosmic tapestry of creation, they embrace the challenges that lie ahead, knowing that their love will guide them through the darkest of nights and lead them towards the dawn of a new day.

Trials of the
Celestial Realm

As Shiva and Parvati traverse the celestial realm on their epic journey, they encounter trials that test their resolve and challenge their bond. From the celestial mountains to the cosmic oceans, they face obstacles that threaten to derail their quest for divine union.

Their first trial comes in the form of the Celestial Guardians, mighty beings charged with protecting the realms of the gods. As Shiva and Parvati approach the celestial gates, they are met with skepticism and resistance, for the guardians doubt the sincerity of their love and the purity of their intentions.

Undeterred, Shiva and Parvati stand firm in their resolve, their love shining like a beacon amidst the darkness of doubt and suspicion. With humility and grace, they plead their case before the Celestial Guardians, invoking the power of their divine connection to overcome the barriers that stand in their way.

Moved by the depth of their devotion and the purity of their hearts, the Celestial Guardians relent, granting Shiva and Parvati passage through the celestial gates. And so, with their first trial overcome, the divine couple continues on their journey, their spirits undaunted by the challenges that lie ahead.

Their next trial comes in the form of the Cosmic Tempest, a raging storm that threatens to engulf them in its fury. As lightning flashes and thunder roars, Shiva and Parvati find themselves tested to their limits, their faith in each other their only anchor amidst the chaos.

With unwavering determination, they press on, their love serving as a shield against the tempest's wrath. Together, they weather the storm, emerging on the other side stronger and more resolute than ever before. And so, with each trial they face, Shiva and Parvati's bond grows stronger, their love shining ever brighter amidst the darkness that surrounds them.

As they journey deeper into the celestial realm, Shiva and Parvati encounter challenges that push them to the brink of their abilities. Yet, with each obstacle they overcome, they emerge victorious, their love triumphant over all adversity.

And so, as Shiva and Parvati's epic journey continues, they remain steadfast in their determination to unite their souls in eternal love, their spirits undaunted by the trials that lie ahead.

Guardians of the
Cosmic Gates

As Shiva and Parvati venture deeper into the celestial realm, they come upon the fabled Gates of Cosmic Harmony, guarded by ancient sentinels whose duty is to ensure the balance of the cosmos is maintained. These guardians, known as the Keepers of Balance, stand tall and resolute, their eyes ablaze with the wisdom of the ages.

Approaching the gates, Shiva and Parvati are greeted by the solemn gaze of the Keepers, who scrutinize them with an intensity that pierces the depths of their souls. Sensing the weight of their presence, Shiva and Parvati bow respectfully, acknowledging the guardians' authority and wisdom.

The Keepers, guardians of cosmic order, inquire into the purpose of Shiva and Parvati's journey, seeking to discern the sincerity of their intentions and the purity of their hearts. With humility and grace, the divine couple recounts their quest for union, their love transcending the boundaries of mortal existence and uniting them in a bond that echoes through the ages.

Impressed by the depth of their devotion and the purity of their souls, the Keepers of Balance nod in silent approval, their resolve softened by the sincerity of Shiva and Parvati's love. With a gesture of acceptance, they grant the divine couple passage through the gates, bestowing upon them their blessings for a safe and prosperous journey.

And so, with the gates of cosmic harmony now open before them, Shiva and Parvati continue on their epic journey, their spirits buoyed by the knowledge that they have earned the trust and respect of the guardians of the celestial realm. With each step they take, each challenge they face, they draw ever closer to the fulfillment of their divine purpose - the union of their souls in eternal love.

As they pass through the gates, Shiva and Parvati feel a sense of awe and wonder wash over them, as if they are stepping into a realm beyond the bounds of mortal understanding. Ahead lies a path fraught with peril and uncertainty, but they press on undaunted, their love guiding them through the darkness and illuminating the way forward.

And so, as Shiva and Parvati's epic journey unfolds amidst the celestial wonders of the cosmos, they remain steadfast in their determination to overcome whatever obstacles may lie ahead, their spirits undaunted by the challenges that await them.

The Trials of Celestial Realms

As Shiva and Parvati continue their epic journey through the celestial realms, they encounter trials that test their courage, strength, and unwavering commitment to each other. Each challenge they face brings them closer to the realization of their divine purpose, forging their bond ever stronger amidst the cosmic wonders that surround them.

Their next trial unfolds in the form of the Celestial Maze, a labyrinthine puzzle of cosmic proportions that tests not only their intellect but also their ability to navigate the intricate web of fate and destiny. As they venture into the maze, Shiva and Parvati must rely on their intuition and inner guidance to find their way through the twisting passages and hidden chambers that lie ahead.

With each twist and turn, they encounter obstacles and challenges that threaten to confound their progress and lead them astray. But with unwavering determination and a steadfast belief in each other, they press on, their love serving as a guiding light in the darkness that surrounds them.

As they navigate the labyrinth, Shiva and Parvati encounter manifestations of their deepest fears and insecurities, forcing them to confront the shadows that lurk within their own hearts. Yet, with courage and determination, they face these challenges head-on, emerging stronger and more resilient with each obstacle they overcome.

Finally, after what feels like an eternity, Shiva and Parvati emerge from the Celestial Maze, victorious in their quest to unravel its mysteries and unlock its secrets. With a sense of triumph and accomplishment, they continue on their journey, their spirits buoyed by the knowledge that they have overcome yet another trial on the path to their ultimate destiny.

But their journey is far from over, for the celestial realms hold many more challenges and adventures that await them. With each trial they face, Shiva and Parvati grow ever closer to the realization of their divine purpose, their love serving as a beacon of hope and inspiration amidst the cosmic wonders that surround them.

And so, as Shiva and Parvati's epic journey continues to unfold amidst the celestial realms, they remain steadfast in their determination to overcome whatever obstacles may lie ahead, their spirits undaunted by the challenges that await them.

Guardians of the Cosmic Oceans

In their epic journey through the celestial realms, Shiva and Parvati come upon the vast expanse of the Cosmic Oceans, where the boundaries between time and space blur into infinity. Here, they encounter the enigmatic Guardians of the Cosmic Oceans, ancient beings whose wisdom is as deep as the depths they inhabit.

Approaching the shores of the Cosmic Oceans, Shiva and Parvati are greeted by the solemn presence of the Guardians, whose eyes gleam with the wisdom of countless ages. Sensing the weight of their gaze, the divine couple bows in reverence, acknowledging the guardians' authority and seeking their guidance on their journey.

The Guardians, custodians of the cosmic waters, inquire into the purpose of Shiva and Parvati's journey, seeking to discern the purity of their intentions and the sincerity of their hearts. With humility and grace, the divine couple recounts their quest for union, their love transcending the boundaries of mortal existence and leading them on a path towards divine enlightenment.

Impressed by the depth of their devotion and the purity of their souls, the Guardians nod in silent approval, their presence a reassuring beacon amidst the vastness of the cosmic waters. With a gesture of acceptance, they bestow upon Shiva and Parvati their blessings for a safe and prosperous journey through the depths of the Cosmic Oceans.

And so, with the guidance of the Guardians, Shiva and Parvati set sail upon the cosmic waters, their spirits buoyed by the knowledge that they are not alone on their journey. As they navigate the currents of the Cosmic Oceans, they encounter wonders beyond imagination - celestial beings and cosmic wonders that stir their souls and fill them with awe.

Yet, amidst the beauty and majesty of the cosmic waters, Shiva and Parvati also face challenges that test their resolve and challenge their faith. From the treacherous storms that rage across the surface to the hidden dangers that lurk in the depths below, they must rely on their love and trust in each other to guide them safely through the trials that lie ahead.

And so, as Shiva and Parvati's epic journey continues through the Cosmic Oceans, they remain steadfast in their determination to overcome whatever obstacles may arise, their spirits undaunted by the challenges that await them.

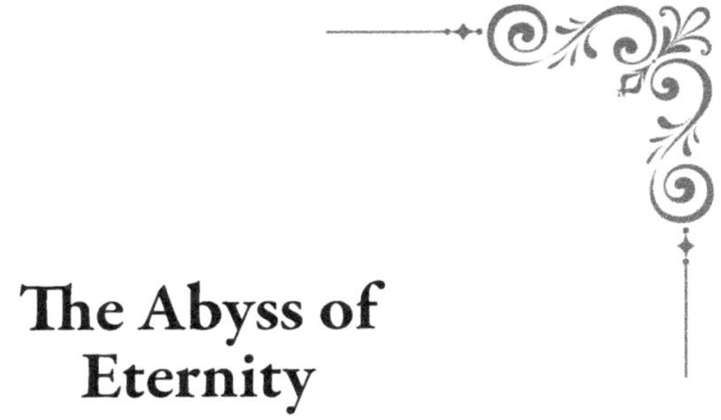

The Abyss of Eternity

As Shiva and Parvati journey deeper into the Cosmic Oceans, they come upon a realm shrouded in mystery and darkness - the Abyss of Eternity. Here, the waters run deep and cold, and the currents are swift and unforgiving. It is a place where the boundaries between reality and illusion blur, and the very fabric of existence seems to unravel.

Navigating the treacherous waters of the Abyss, Shiva and Parvati find themselves confronted by the echoes of their deepest fears and insecurities. In this realm of shadows and illusions, they are forced to confront the shadows that lurk within their own hearts, facing their inner demons with courage and determination.

As they journey deeper into the Abyss, Shiva and Parvati encounter manifestations of their past traumas and regrets, each one a reminder of the challenges they have faced and the obstacles they have overcome. Yet, with each trial they face, they emerge stronger and more resilient, their love serving as a beacon of hope amidst the darkness that surrounds them.

But the Abyss of Eternity is not without its dangers, for lurking within its depths are ancient beings of darkness and despair, whose malevolent presence threatens to consume all who dare to venture too close. With each passing moment, Shiva and Parvati feel the weight of the Abyss pressing down upon them, testing the limits of their endurance and resolve.

Yet, even in the face of such overwhelming darkness, Shiva and Parvati refuse to succumb to despair, drawing strength from their love and trust in each other. With unwavering determination, they press on, their spirits undaunted by the shadows that threaten to engulf them.

And so, as Shiva and Parvati's epic journey through the Abyss of Eternity continues, they remain steadfast in their determination to overcome whatever challenges may lie ahead, their love shining like a guiding star amidst the darkness that surrounds them.

For theirs is a love that transcends the boundaries of time and space, a bond that has endured through the ages and will continue to shine bright long after the stars themselves have faded into oblivion.

Poem: Journey of Souls

In the vast expanse where stars do roam,
    Two souls embarked on a cosmic home.
Shiva, the lord of timeless grace,
Parvati, his beloved, their destinies embrace.
Through realms of light and shadows deep,
Their journey took them, their love to keep.
Amidst celestial wonders, their spirits soared,
Infinite love, forever adored.
Across celestial oceans, they sailed with pride,
Through trials and tribulations, side by side.
Their bond, a beacon in the cosmic night,
Guiding them through darkness, towards the light.
In the depths of the abyss, where shadows dwell,
They faced their fears, their souls to quell.
With courage and love, they pressed on through,
Their hearts entwined, their spirits true.
Through realms of time and space untold,
Their journey continued, their love to behold.
For in each other's arms, they found their home,
Two souls united, forever to roam.
And so, their journey of souls unfurled,

Through cosmic wonders, across the world.
For in the dance of creation, they found their fate,
Two souls intertwined, eternal mates.
In the tapestry of stars, their love did shine,
A testament to the divine design.
For in the journey of souls, they found their grace,
Two hearts united, in a timeless embrace.

The Divine Union: A Journey of Love

In the realm where love's flames brightly burn,
  Two souls entwined, a sacred turn.
Parvati, the goddess of beauty and grace,
Shiva, the lord, his divine embrace.
Through cosmic wonders, their journey unfurls,
In each other's arms, they find their pearls.
Every step they take, a tale untold,
In their love's embrace, the universe enfold.
In the depths of their hearts, a love so pure,
In every moment, their souls allure.
From celestial heights to mortal lands,
Their love shines bright, like golden sands.
In the tapestry of time, their story weaves,
A saga of love, the heart believes.
For in each other's gaze, they find their light,
In the depths of their love, their souls unite.
Through trials and tribulations, their love prevails,
In the cosmic dance, their bond unveils.
For Parvati and Shiva, a journey divine,
In the union of souls, their love will shine.

Conclusion

In the grand finale of their cosmic odyssey, Shiva and Parvati stand atop Mount Kailash, the pinnacle of divine realization and the culmination of their epic journey. Here, amidst the celestial splendor of the highest peak, they gaze upon the vast expanse of creation spread out before them, their hearts overflowing with love and gratitude for the wondrous adventure they have shared.

As they reflect on the trials and triumphs of their journey, Shiva and Parvati are filled with a deep sense of reverence for the cosmic forces that have guided their path and the divine grace that has sustained them through every challenge. They understand that their union is not just a bond between two souls, but a sacred covenant forged in the fires of destiny and tempered by the trials of existence.

In the presence of the cosmic deities who have witnessed their journey, Shiva and Parvati offer prayers of gratitude and devotion, acknowledging the role that each being has played in shaping their destiny and guiding them towards enlightenment. They recognize that their love is not just a personal affair, but a cosmic phenomenon that resonates with the very essence of creation itself.

As they stand hand in hand, bathed in the celestial light of Mount Kailash, Shiva and Parvati pledge their eternal love and devotion to each other, vowing to honor and cherish their union for all eternity. In this sacred moment, they transcend the limitations of mortal existence, merging their souls in a divine embrace that transcends time and space.

And so, as the sun sets on their epic journey, Shiva and Parvati descend from Mount Kailash, their hearts filled with the radiant glow of divine love. As they return to the mortal realm, they carry with them the wisdom and grace of their celestial adventure, sharing the light of their love with all beings who cross their path.

For Shiva and Parvati, their journey may have reached its conclusion, but their love will continue to shine bright, illuminating the hearts of all who seek the divine within themselves. In their union, they have found the true essence of existence – a love that transcends all boundaries and unites all beings in the cosmic dance of creation.

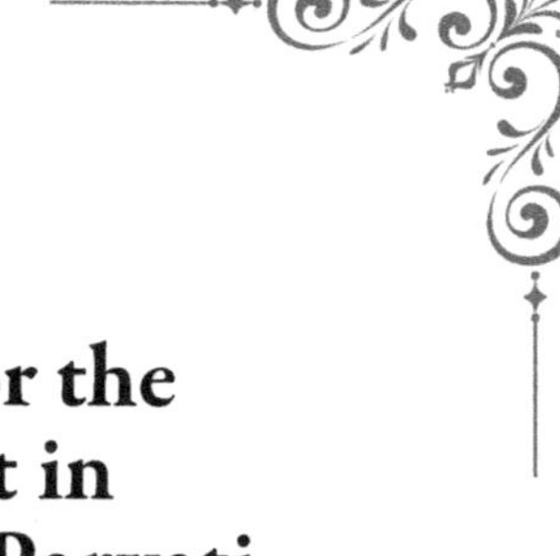

Apology for the Oversight in Referring to Parvati and Lord Shiva

Dear Readers,

I hope this message finds you well. I am writing to address an oversight in my recent book, "Divine Union: The Eternal Love Story of Shiva and Parvati," where I referred to Maa Parvati simply as "Parvati" and Lord Shiva as "Shiv" without acknowledging their divine titles.

I deeply regret this mistake and sincerely apologize for any offense or misunderstanding it may have caused. It was not my intention to diminish the reverence and respect due to Maa Parvati and Lord Shiva, who are revered as divine beings in Hindu mythology.

I recognize the importance of honoring their divine status by using their proper titles, Maa Parvati and Lord Shiva, in this book. I acknowledge the significance of their names and titles in representing their roles as divine figures in Hinduism, and I apologize for any oversight in this regard.

As an author, I take full responsibility for the oversight and assure you that I will strive to be more mindful and respectful in my writing in the future. I am committed to upholding the highest standards of accuracy and sensitivity in all my literary endeavors.

Once again, I apologize for any offense caused and thank you for your understanding and forgiveness.

Sincerely,

Mrigendra Bharti

Heartfelt Gratitude
to Our Readers

Dear Esteemed Readers,

As the author of "Divine Union: The Eternal Love Story of Shiva and Parvati," I am deeply humbled and grateful for the overwhelming support and appreciation you have shown for my work.

Your enthusiasm and encouragement have been the driving force behind this literary journey, and I am truly honored to have had the opportunity to share the timeless tale of love and devotion between Shiva and Parvati with you.

Your feedback and insights have been invaluable, and I am deeply appreciative of the time and thought you have invested in engaging with my book. Your passion for literature and dedication to exploring the depths of human emotion inspire me to continue writing and sharing stories that touch the heart and soul.

I am committed to upholding the highest standards of storytelling and creativity in all my future endeavors, and I look forward to embarking on new literary adventures with you by my side.

Once again, thank you from the bottom of my heart for your unwavering support and enthusiasm. It is truly a privilege to have you as readers, and I am immensely grateful for the opportunity to connect with each and every one of you through the power of storytelling.

With deepest gratitude and warmest regards,
Mrigendra Bharti

Har Har Mahadev

About the Author

Mrigendra Bharti, born on June 29, 2004, in South Delhi, India, is a multifaceted individual recognized as the owner of Mrigendra Bharti Group InfoTech India Co. Pvt Ltd. Beyond his entrepreneurial endeavors, he is a distinguished music producer, director, and a budding writer.

Embarking on his professional journey at a young age, Mrigendra Bharti's visionary leadership has led to the establishment of several successful ventures, including Croma Music Series Entertainment, Sellbrochure, Fauget Innovative, and more.

What sets Mrigendra apart is his early initiation into the world of business. His foray into the unknown realms of entrepreneurship began during his 10th-grade years, where he delved into the music industry. This initial venture laid the foundation for subsequent achievements, showcasing his dedication and resilience.

Having honed his skills in music, Mrigendra Bharti not only demonstrated significant growth in his craft but also expanded his professional network. His passion extends beyond music, encompassing app and website development, as well as graphic design.

Fueled by his creative aspirations, Mrigendra established the Mrigendra Bharti Group, a company specializing in website and app development. Currently, he collaborates with a dedicated team, collectively working on ambitious projects that promise innovation and excellence.

Mrigendra's journey serves as an inspiration, particularly for today's students, highlighting the potential of youthful determination and the ability to transform innovative ideas into successful businesses. As he continues to make strides in various domains, Mrigendra Bharti remains a dynamic force, contributing vibrancy to the realms of business, music, and technology.

Read more at https://www.imwriter-mrigendra.rf.gd.

www.ingramcontent.com/pod-product-compliance
Lightning Source LLC
Chambersburg PA
CBHW071450130726
47997CB00006B/2313